Mia
and the Daisy Dance

HOORAY!

Kylie + Emily

can read this book!

ISBN 978-0-06-173305-5

US $3.99 / $4.99 CAN

www.harpercollinschildrens.com

BOOK NEWS, GAMES, CONTESTS, AND MORE

9 780061 733055

50399

13 03

S

Dear Parent:
Your child's love of reading starts here!

Every child learns to read in a different way and at his or her own speed. Some go back and forth between reading levels and read favorite books again and again. Others read through each level in order. You can help your young reader improve and become more confident by encouraging his or her own interests and abilities. From books your child reads with you to the first books he or she reads alone, there are I Can Read Books for every stage of reading:

SHARED READING
Basic language, word repetition, and whimsical illustrations, ideal for sharing with your emergent reader

BEGINNING READING
Short sentences, familiar words, and simple concepts for children eager to read on their own

READING WITH HELP
Engaging stories, longer sentences, and language play for developing readers

READING ALONE
Complex plots, challenging vocabulary, and high-interest topics for the independent reader

ADVANCED READING
Short paragraphs, chapters, and exciting themes for the perfect bridge to chapter books

I Can Read Books have introduced children to the joy of reading since 1957. Featuring award-winning authors and illustrators and a fabulous cast of beloved characters, I Can Read Books set the standard for beginning readers.

A lifetime of discovery begins with the magical words "I Can Read!"

Visit www.icanread.com for information
on enriching your child's reading experience.

I Can Read Book® is a trademark of HarperCollins Publishers.

Mia and the Daisy Dance
Copyright © 2012 by HarperCollins Publishers
All rights reserved. Manufactured in China.
No part of this book may be used or reproduced in any manner whatsoever without written permission except in the case of brief quotations embodied in critical articles and reviews. For information address HarperCollins Children's Books, a division of HarperCollins Publishers, 10 East 53rd Street, New York, NY 10022.
www.icanread.com
Library of Congress Cataloging-in-Publication Data is available.
ISBN 978-0-06-173306-2 (trade bdg.)—ISBN 978-0-06-173305-5 (pbk.)
Typography by Sean Boggs
13 14 15 16 SCP 10 9 8 7 6 5 4 3 ❖ First Edition

I Can Read!™

SHARED
My
First
READING

Mia

and the
Daisy Dance

by Robin Farley
pictures by Aleksey and Olga Ivanov

HARPER

An Imprint of HarperCollinsPublishers

"Class," sings
Miss Bird.
"Good news!

The Daisy Dance is soon.

It is a big show!"

Mia jumps for joy!
Each dancer gets
to do a solo.

Mia will drop flowers,
and Anna will twirl
onstage!

Miss Bird teaches
the new dance.

But Anna does not dance.

She does not want to.

She wants to go home.

Mia is worried.

She wants the Daisy Dance
to go well.

Anna looks scared.

Mia wants to help.

But how?

At home, Mia practices
the new dance
over and over.

Mia hears
thump, thump, thump
on the door.

"Who is it?"
she asks.

"Will you help me
learn my steps?"
asks Anna.

"I have never done
a twirl," says Anna.
"Have you?"

Mia smiles.

Mia knows how it feels
to be scared.

"Yes!" says Mia.
"I will dance with you,
and we will both learn!"

Mia twirls and stops.

She hops and kicks.